Cute and Crazy Cats

with activities
and puzzles

Illustrations by Jean Rudegeair
Cover Photograph by Robert Cushman Hayes

ap **Antioch Publishing Company**
Yellow Springs, Ohio 45387

Copyright © 1983 by Antioch Publishing Company
Made in the United States of America

Hank's Hungry!

Help Hank get home for supper. Look out for trouble on the way.

Feline Friends and Foes

Find a friend or foe for each of the famous felines below.

1. GARFIELD
2. PINK PANTHER
3. CALICO CAT
4. TIGGER
5. TOM
6. AZRAEL
7. LITTLE FIGARO
8. CUSTARD
9. SYLVESTER
10. THE CAT IN THE HAT

A. Strawberry Shortcake
B. Gargamel
C. Jerry
D. Tweety Bird
E. Odie
F. Gingham Dog
G. Thing One and Thing Two
H. Winnie the Pooh
I. Inspector Clouseau
J. Pinocchio

Photograph by ANIMALS, ANIMALS / Robert Pearcy

Kinds of Kats

Read forward, backward, up and down, and diagonally. Find the words listed below.

```
        D O                 M L
      N M O B             O A U E
    A R T C M A D A T Y A U S S O
  L Y Z I L W E O F E B Z E H U I R
R N E T G A M O S A L B M A Q O W K O
P A L L E S H O R T H A I R L H I C R
S H L U R S J G T A I T R E A T I H K
  T A C D L I W N S F C A L T L A R
  N A I S R E P O B B D E A S T
    F R I E N D L Y N C U
      B L A X S
```

WORDS TO FIND

TOM, TABBY, CALICO, ALLEY, HOUSE, FRIENDLY, TIGER, SHORTHAIR, LONGHAIR, KITTEN, SIAMESE, FAT, PERSIAN, DOMESTIC, WILDCAT, LAZY

6

Photograph by Jean Wentworth

Kitty Crossword

CLUES

1. A favorite treat for kitty

2. Her quiet padded feet

3. Something on her face that helps guide her

4. What she says to you each morning

5. How her fur feels when you pet her

6. Something she is careful not to get caught in the door

Photograph by Betty Powell

Cat Got Your Tongue?

Try saying these phrases three times . . . fast!

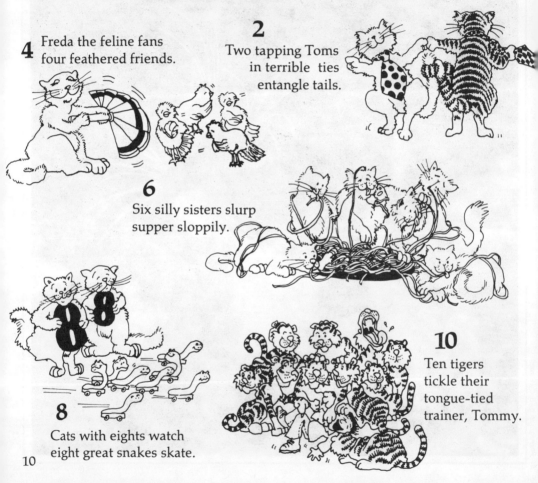

4 Freda the feline fans four feathered friends.

2 Two tapping Toms in terrible ties entangle tails.

6 Six silly sisters slurp supper sloppily.

8 Cats with eights watch eight great snakes skate.

10 Ten tigers tickle their tongue-tied trainer, Tommy.

Find 30 things hidden in this **CROWD OF CATS** that begin with the letter "C." Do not count the cats!

Photograph by Robert Cushman Hayes

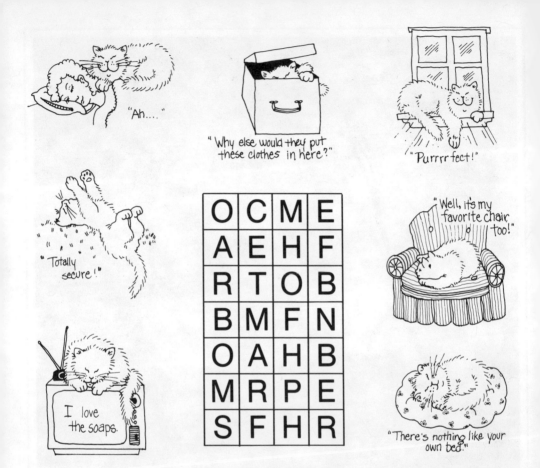

O	C	M	E
A	E	H	F
R	T	O	B
B	M	F	N
O	A	H	B
M	R	P	E
S	F	H	R

Cross out each letter that appears in the box three times.
The letters that are left make a title for this page.

Photograph by Dorothy Holby

— FELINE FUNNIES —

When is it bad luck to have a black cat follow you?
When you are a mouse

Which side of a cat has the most fur?
The outside

What did the cat say after it met the mouse?
Burp!

What did the cat say to the flea?
"Don't bug me!"

What's worse than raining cats and dogs?
Hailing taxis

What did the 500 pound mouse say to the cat?
"Here Kitty, Kitty! Here Kitty, Kitty!"

Photograph by Robert Cushman Hayes

Tricks 'n Treats

Unscramble these sayings. Just write the letter of the alphabet that comes *before* each letter in the mixed-up messages.

B USJDL B EBZ
LFFQT UIF
DBU BXBZ!

EPO'U DSZ PWFS
TQJMMFE NJML.
MBQ JU VQ!

18

Photograph by H. Reinhard/Bruce Coleman, Inc.

copy cats

Find the twins. Two cats are exactly alike.

Photograph by Jean Wentworth

Cute and Crazy

How many words can you make using the letters in the words CUTE AND CRAZY?
There are more than 50 new words hiding in these 3 words.